MAX AND MARLA

ARE HAVING A PICNIC

ALEXANDRA BOIGER

G. P. PUTNAM'S SONS

To my sisters Martina and Ursula, with love.

Special Thanks:
I'd like to thank some very special people: Marcia Wernick, who supported me all the way;
Jen Besser for giving me wings and sharing her wisdom; and Cecilia Yung for her protective
fierceness and ability to keep me grounded. Thank you also to Annie Hirshman for her wonderful
design work on the first *Max and Marla*, and to Dave Kopka for his beautiful work on this book.

G. P. PUTNAM'S SONS
an imprint of Penguin Random House LLC
375 Hudson Street
New York, NY 10014

Library of Congress Cataloging-in-Publication Data
Names: Boiger, Alexandra, author, illustrator.
Title: Max and Marla are having a picnic / Alexandra Boiger.
Description: New York, NY : G. P. Putnam's Sons, [2018].
Summary: "As Max and Marla set out for the perfect picnic, they learn getting along
isn't always easy, but best friends can't stay mad for long"—Provided by publisher.
Identifiers: LCCN 2017016571 | ISBN 9780399175053 (hardback)
ISBN 9780698196469 (ebook) | ISBN 9780698196476 (ebook)
Subjects: | CYAC: Best friends—Fiction. | Friendship—Fiction. | Picnics—Fiction.
Birds—Fiction. | BISAC: JUVENILE FICTION / Imagination & Play. | JUVENILE
FICTION / Social Issues / Friendship. | JUVENILE FICTION / Animals / General.
Classification: LCC PZ7.1.B65 May 2018 | DDC [E]—dc23
LC record available at https://lccn.loc.gov/2017016571

Manufactured in China by RR Donnelley Asia Printing Solutions Ltd.
ISBN 9780399175053
1 3 5 7 9 10 8 6 4 2

Design by Annie Hirshman and Dave Kopka. Text set in Brandon Grotesque.
The art for this book was rendered in watercolor and ink on Fabriano paper, then
scanned and further overworked in Photoshop by adding spot textures and colors.

MAX and MARLA are waiting for the first
sunny day of spring. The news tells them:
Heavy showers all throughout today . . .

. . . warm and sunny tomorrow.

You see, each year, these two best friends
celebrate the beginning of spring with
a picnic extraordinaire down by the lake.

"We'll make all of our favorite dishes. Right, Marla? Homemade lemonade, potato salad, cheese and baguette, vanilla pudding with fresh strawberries . . . and Grandma's special cake: a gugelhupf."

"Did I miss anything?"

No, Max, you didn't.
But time is of the essence.

"Marla?
MARLA!!"

Oh well.

They manage to finish it all just fine.
Even *with* Marla's help.

The weatherwoman
had promised a
perfect spring day.

And she was right!
It's sunny, it's warm—
and it is about time.

This is going to be **the best picnic EVER!**

Max and Marla's tummies begin to rumble.

"Hmm . . . we are missing
just one thing," says Max.
"I will be back in a minute."

Marla is very good at waiting.

And napping.

This day is perfect!

Max is finally back.

"These flowers are for you . . ."

"Marla, what has happened here?
You have started without me!"

"LOOK! There are food thieves at work!"

Marla and Max don't feel like staying any longer.
They don't even want to look at each other.

This was not a good day.

"*Max Pan and the Lost Owls* is Marla's favorite book," thinks Max.
"She loves it when I read bedtime stories to her."

"Marla must be tired."

"She always giggles
when I brush her beak.
Marla must be very hungry!
I am very hungry!"

Max has an idea . . .

"These flowers are for you, Marla."

How fitting that Marla's favorite color is blue.

Max and Marla are having the best picnic ever!
It's cozy, it's warm, and it is heavenly scrumptious.